The Elephantom

For Nate

First U.S. edition 2015

Library of Congress Catalog Card Number 2014939357
ISBN 978-0-7636-7591-2

15 16 17 18 19 20 TLF 10 9 8 7 6 5 4 3 2 1

Printed in Dongguan, Guangdong, China

This book was typeset in Aunt Mildred MVB and Providence-Sans.
The illustrations were done in watercolor.

TEMPLAR BOOKS

an imprint of
Candlewick Press
99 Dover Street
Somerville, Massachusetts 02144
www.candlewick.com

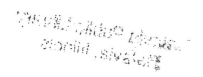

The ElePhANtom

Ross Collins

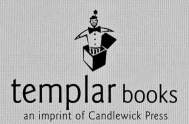

templar books
an imprint of Candlewick Press

We have an elephantom.

He turned up one Tuesday
after dinner.

To be honest, he's starting to bug me.

He keeps me awake at night . . .

and gets me into trouble.

"It's spinach sandwiches for you, young lady, until you stop hogging all the peanut butter."

On Fridays he invites all his friends over.

I can't say it's the highlight of MY week. . . .

My parents don't seem to notice phantom elephants.

Dad hasn't even realized that it's my room that always smells like dung.

"New perfume, darling? What an . . .

nteresting aroma."

And whenever I try to tell Mom,
she doesn't take me seriously.

"That's nice, dear—
why don't you go and tell
your grandma?"

"Grandma, we have an elephantom."

I knew Grandma would believe me—she has lots of ghost pets.

But when I explained that the elephantom
was a bit of a nuisance and I didn't
want him anymore,

Grandma knew just what to do.

Spectral & Son

PURVEYORS of ODDITIES

564 Collywobble Court

WALK-INS WELCOME

She rummaged around and
found an old card.

"Mr. Spectral will help you out,"
she said.

It took me four hours and thirty-seven minutes
to find the shop.

Inside, it was dark and musty.
Mr. Spectral's stock was . . . unusual.

"I want to get rid of an elephantom,"
I said.

Mr. Spectral nodded.

"I have fifty cents,"
I said.

Mr. Spectral
smiled . . .

and gave me
a box.

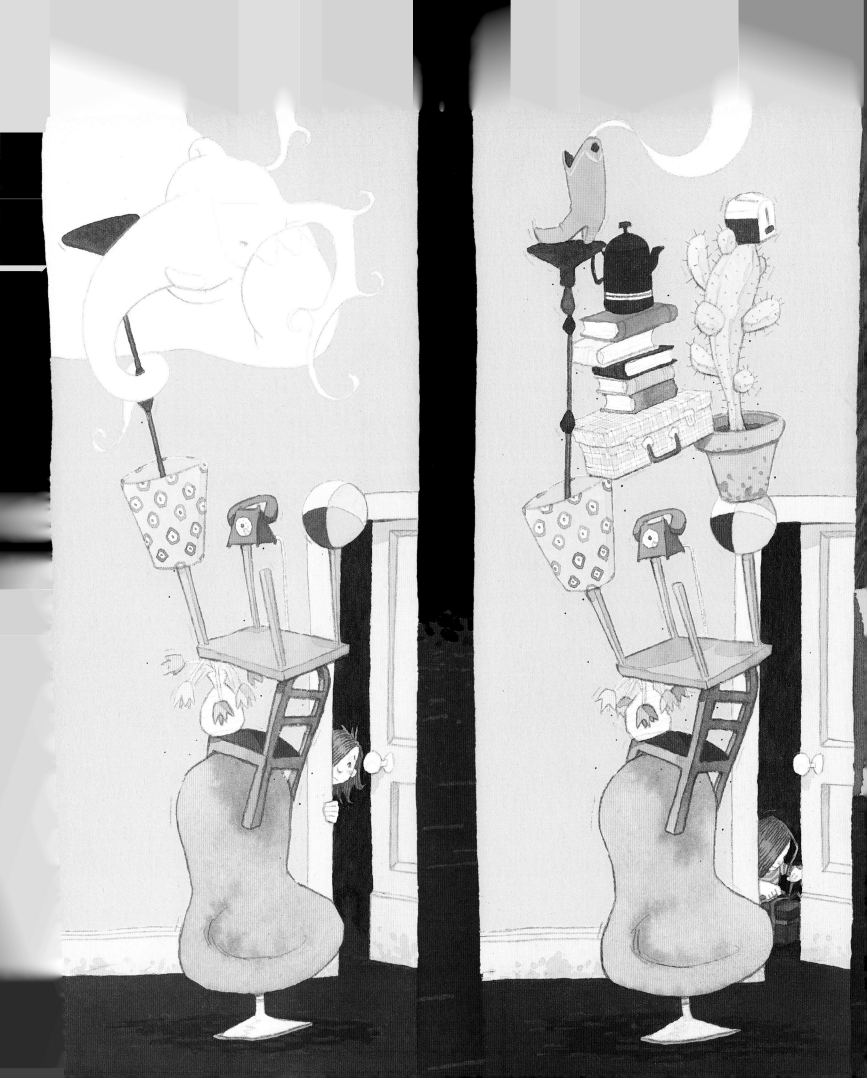

We don't have an elephantom anymore . . .